DREAMWORKS®

KUNG FU
PANDA
LEGENDS OF
AWESOMENESS
nickelodeon.

TWO TO KUNG FU

adapted by Tracey West

Simon Spotlight
New York   London   Toronto   Sydney   New Delhi

SIMON SPOTLIGHT
An imprint of Simon & Schuster Children's Publishing Division
1230 Avenue of the Americas, New York, New York 10020
Kung Fu Panda Legends of Awesomeness © 2014 Viacom International Inc. NICKELODEON and all related logos are trademarks of Viacom International Inc. Based on the feature film Kung Fu Panda © 2008 DreamWorks Animation L.L.C. All Rights Reserved.
All rights reserved, including the right of reproduction in whole or in part in any form.
SIMON SPOTLIGHT and colophon are registered trademarks of Simon & Schuster, Inc.
For information about special discounts for bulk purchases, please contact Simon & Schuster Special Sales at 1-866-506-1949 or business@simonandschuster.com.
Manufactured in the United States of America 0214 OFF
First Edition 10 9 8 7 6 5 4 3 2
ISBN 978-1-4424-9992-8 (pbk)
ISBN 978-1-4424-9993-5 (hc)
ISBN 978-1-4424-9994-2 (eBook)

CHAIN REACTION

CHAPTER ONE

"The two legendary warriors strode bravely toward danger," Po said. "Cutting through the thick fog like it was . . . soup. Dangerous, evil . . . soup."

Tigress sighed. Po had not stopped talking since they had left the Jade Palace.

"The two best friends had been through much that day—an epic march, a treacherous scouting mission. But they were about to face the most fearsome part yet," Po went on. "Mr. Yang!"

They opened the shop door . . . and stepped in front of a short pig wearing glasses.

"They must pay Mr. Yang, the grumpy statue-cleaner, and return with their prize," Po said, "Shifu's favorite ruby-encrusted statue of Oogway, which had grown dirty from the fearsome assault of time . . . and dust . . . and dried rice bits dropped on it." (By Po, of course, but he left out that part.)

"Po!" Tigress yelled as they hoisted the statue onto a stretcher so they could carry it. "Quit daydreaming out loud!"

They left the shop and carried the statue outside. Rain poured down on them as they made their way back to the Jade Palace.

"Well, I wouldn't do it if you'd talk to me a little," Po said, pouting.

"Po, we're on a mission," Tigress reminded him in her steady voice.

"Okay, okay then," Po agreed. "Just super-important mission stuff."

Tigress nodded. "Fine."

"Like . . . what's your favorite color?" Po asked.

Tigress sighed again, but that didn't stop Po.

"This is hard," Po said. "They're all so great. Why can't there be one color that's so much more awesome than the others? It could be a color you've never heard of, like 'floogoo.'"

Tigress stopped and glared at Po. "I have a rule about idle chit chat. I don't do it."

"You have a rule about everything!" Po complained as they started walking again. "If we're

going to be best friends like the way I dreamed about since I was five, you're going to have to loosen up."

At that moment, Po and Tigress lost their grip on the stretcher. The statue wobbled and started to fall.

Tigress quickly ran next to Po and put her paws on the statue. "Push!"

Clank!

A handcuff snapped around Tigress's left paw. Another cuff snapped around Po's right paw. A thick chain connected the two cuffs, linking Tigress and Po.

They spun around—and saw a group of Croc Bandits standing in front of them! Their leader, Fung, wore a metal helmet on his head.

He turned to his crew. "Take the statue and get the ruby."

"You'll take nothing!" Tigress cried. She jumped on a rock and aimed a punch at one of the bandits. But she didn't get very far. The chain

didn't reach far enough. She went flying back-
ward.

Po launched into a kung-fu pose.

"Shak-a-boo . . . ow!"

His foot got wrapped up in the chain, and he
fell flat on his face. The Crocs chuckled. Then the
bandits charged at Tigress and Po, backing them

up to the edge of a steep cliff. They watched helplessly as two of the Crocs ran off with the statue.

"Spears!" Fung ordered.

The bandits drew their long, sharp weapons.

"I'm saving the statue!" Tigress cried. "We can take them."

"Good idea," Po said. "But first, let's not die. Don't be mad."

Tigress was puzzled. "Why would I be . . ." But then she realized what Po had in mind. "Oh no!"

Po jumped off the cliff, taking Tigress with him!

CHAPTER TWO

A aaaaaaaaaaaaaah!"
   The two warriors screamed as they plunged down . . . and down . . . and down.

   The chain got caught on a tree branch sticking out of the side of the cliff. It stopped their fall, but the two ends of the chain swung back and forth. Po and Tigress knocked into each other like a pair of nunchucks.

   Then . . . *crack*! The tree branch broke, sending them plummeting down once again.

"Aaaaaaaaaaaaah!"

They crashed to the floor of the bamboo forest below.

Tigress leaped to her feet. "I can't believe we lost the statue . . . and the ruby."

"Oh, did we?" Po asked. He opened his paw, revealing the glittering red ruby. "I grabbed it before the crocs ran off with the statue. I guess they were too busy punching me to notice. Losers."

"But when they do notice, they'll be after us," Tigress pointed out. "Let's head that way."

Tigress took off through the forest, dragging Po behind her.

"We're going to get that statue back," Po said.

Tigress nodded. "We can't do anything till we get these chains off."

Suddenly spears whizzed by. The Croc Bandits were back. Po and Tigress followed a dirt path up

13

a hill to a temple surrounded by a stone wall. They bolted the wooden gate behind them.

Tigress scanned the area. A huge metal bell hung from two posts. Her eyes lit up.

She led Po to the big bell, and he stood right under it. He nervously looked up at the heavy metal object hanging above him. Tigress gave the post next to her a powerful push. The bell slammed down, covering Po and hitting the ground with a loud clang. Tigress had hoped the heavy bell could break the chain. But it was still in one piece.

With another push, she knocked the bell off Po. The sound of the bell still rang in his ears.

"DID IT WORK?" he yelled.

"Shhh," Tigress warned.

"WHAT? I CAN'T HEAR ANYTHING. WHAT WORDS AM I SAYING?" Po shouted.

Po's loud voice brought the Crocs right to them. They crashed into the wooden gate. Tigress knew they could break through in seconds.

"Brace yourself," she told Po.

"Really?" Po asked.

Tigress grabbed the chain with both hands. She swung it around and around, with Po flying at the end. When she had built up enough speed . . .

Smash! She pounded Po into the stone wall behind them. Po sailed through the hole, and Tigress jumped after him.

They were just in time. As soon as they got through the wall, the Croc Bandits burst through the gate.

CHAPTER THREE

Po and Tigress ran until they lost the Crocs again. Exhausted, they sat down at the base of a big tree.

"I can't think," Tigress said. "I haven't eaten all day."

Po looked up into the tree and saw an apple hanging from a high branch. He climbed up onto the tree branch. *Snap!* It broke underneath him.

The chain yanked Tigress up as Po fell down. She bonked her head on the branch.

"Panda!" she yelled angrily. "All I wanted was something to . . ." Then she noticed the apple. It had fallen right into her paw. "Thanks, Po."

Tigress was in a better mood after that. As the sun set, Tigress built a fire. Po found a hole in the tree that was filled with honey. He dipped his paw in it and licked it.

Tigress looked up from the piece of wood she was whittling with her sharp claw. "Bees produce more than they eat," she said.

Po was impressed. "You know a lot of stuff!" Not only was Tigress a great fighter, but she was smart, too.

"Um, can I ask you something?" Po said carefully. "You wanted to be the Dragon Warrior, didn't you?"

"*Everyone* wanted to be the Dragon Warrior," Tigress replied.

Po sighed. "You think Oogway made the wrong choice."

Tigress looked away from Po.

"Oookay," Po said, trying to shake off the awkward moment. He picked up some sticks from the ground, grabbing the stick Tigress had been whittling. "Fire's getting a little low."

He tossed everything into the fire.

"Po!" Tigress cried. "I was carving a key to get the shackles opened! I worked for hours on that thing!"

"I thought it was firewood," Po said.

"You didn't *think* at all!" Tigress snapped. "You never do, *Dragon Warrior*." Her voice mocked him as she said those last two words.

Po felt terrible. "I'm just trying to—"

"Do what?" Tigress interrupted. "Lose the statue? Fumble through everything? Is that the Dragon Warrior way? Maybe Oogway *did* make the wrong choice!"

"Tigress, you may be a great warrior," Po said, hurt, "but you stink at friendship. And fun . . . ship. I'm out of here."

Po marched off into the forest. After a few yards he stopped to lick some honey off his paw.

That's when he noticed that he was free.

"The honey must've slipped the cuff off!" he cried. "Is there nothing honey can't do?"

He ran back to the camp. "Tigress! We're free!"

But Tigress was gone.

He got a very un-awesome feeling in his heart. Only one thing could have happened.

The Crocs had taken Tigress!

CHAPTER **FOUR**

Po searched until he found the Croc camp. Peering through the trees, he saw Tigress tied to a post. She was angrily kicking the Crocs with her feet. Then he heard a rumbling sound and saw some Crocs pushing a big wooden weapon into the clearing. It was a huge spinning wheel attached to a platform. Nasty-looking spikes stuck out of the wheel.

Po picked up a rock and chucked it at the nearest Croc guard. It hit a bamboo stalk instead and

ricocheted back to Po, bonking him in the head.

"Ow!" Po yelled.

"There's an intruder in the woods!" Fung yelled. "Find him!"

The Crocs scattered. Po approached Tigress when the coast was clear.

"You okay?" he asked.

"I'm surprised you came back for me," she said. "Thanks."

Po smiled. "Well, it's protocol, you know . . . for friends."

Po jumped up and pounded the post with a mighty kick. The post broke in two, and the ropes slid off Tigress. Quickly, they grabbed the stretcher poles and started to carry away the statue.

The Crocs rushed out of the forest. They surrounded Po and Tigress, poking them with their spears.

"You take half, and I'll take half," Po said.

They set down the stretcher and fought off the Crocs. Po had three Crocs clinging to his back, and three more Crocs clung to Tigress's back. Then Po and Tigress both reached for the statue.

The statue wobbled and toppled over, landing on Tigress. The three Crocs tumbled from her back, and Tigress and the statue rolled across the clearing. The Crocs chased after her.

Po bounced across the clearing, trying to get the Crocs off his back. Tigress clawed her way out from under the statue. One of the Crocs tried to grab it. She deflected him with a powerful kick with both feet.

Tigress grabbed the statue—just as one of the bandits took the empty cuff and chained it to a tall stalk of bamboo. Still carrying the heavy statue, Tigress shimmied up the stalk to lose the Crocs on the ground.

Meanwhile, the other three Croc Bandits surrounded Po.

"Welcome to the *fist*-ival," Po said. "Allow me to punch your tickets!"

He aimed a blow at the nearest Croc—who chomped down on Po's paw.

"Yow!" yelped Po.

The three Crocs jumped him, and they rolled across the clearing. They landed underneath the bamboo stalk just as Tigress, the statue, and the three Crocs chasing her fell to the ground. Po and Tigress were trapped in a tangled mess of Croc Bandits.

"You know what we need?" Po asked. "A plan! We need to do this together."

Clank! Tigress snapped the handcuff on to Po's right paw.

"Why'd you do that?" Po yelled.

CHAPTER **FIVE**

B ecause you're right," Tigress answered.
 Po smiled. He knew what Tigress had in mind.

"Together!" they both yelled at once.

Po and Tigress each thrust a paw into the air. The chain connecting them sent the six Croc Bandits flying.

The Crocs jumped to their feet and hurled their spears. Po and Tigress pulled the chain tightly, and the spears bounced off it. Then they ran forward,

using the chain to knock down a line of Crocs.

Another group of bandits charged them, and Tigress swung the chain in a circle, just like she had done at the temple. With Po at the end, it became the ultimate weapon. He slammed into the charging Crocs.

"How about a little flying-panda style?" Po asked as he took them down.

Po and Tigress heard clapping. Fung stood on his wooden weapon, applauding them.

"Impressive," he said. "But I've got the statue, and you've got the—ruby? No, I don't think so. I have it right here."

He fit the ruby back into the statue. "Look at that! Ha."

He jumped off the wooden platform and began to push the weapon—with the statue on board—out of the clearing. Po and Tigress ran after him. But Fung was heading downhill, and he was picking up speed. He jumped back up onto the platform.

The wheel was spinning like crazy now. If Po and Tigress got too close, the spikes would tear them to pieces. They jumped on top of the wheel, stretching out the chain. With a mighty cry,

they each flew off and grabbed a tree. The chain stretched out, knocking Fung and the statue off the wheel.

Po and Tigress quickly wrapped Fung in the

chain. Then they freed the statue and used the chain like a slingshot to send Fung sailing across the forest. Tigress turned to Po.

"Nice work," she said. She placed her right fist against her flat left palm and bowed respectfully to him. "Oogway did make the right choice, Dragon Warrior."

Po lit up. "Really? Really? I love that you just said that."

As they carried the statue back home, Po sang a song about their adventure.

"The Furious Two! Dragon Warrior and his sidekick after the rampage!"

"Did you say 'sidekick'?" Tigress asked.

"What? No? I mean . . ." Po chuckled awkwardly. "So, what *is* your favorite color?"

Tigress sighed. It was going to be a long trip home!

HOMETOWN HERO

CHAPTER ONE

Po and the Furious Five were training with Master Shifu in the Jade Palace when Zeng, the messenger, flew in with an urgent message for Mantis. He held out a tiny scroll, and Mantis grabbed it.

"What does it say?" Viper asked.

"It says, 'Need your help. Urgent. Hao Ming.'" Mantis gasped.

"What's a *how ming?*" Po asked.

Mantis got a dreamy look in his eyes. "She's

the most beautiful mantis in the world . . . and my ex-fiancée."

"You were going to get married?" Po asked.

"Yeah, but it didn't work out," Mantis explained. "She must be in trouble. I need to go back to my village."

"We'll go with you," Viper offered.

Mantis's antennae wiggled nervously. "Um, you know, my village doesn't really like snakes. Or tigers or monkeys or cranes—it's a really small town. . . ."

He quickly turned and hopped away from the palace.

Po was puzzled. "That's weird. I mean, who wouldn't want to bring the Dragon Warrior back to their hometown?"

"Po, follow Mantis, in case he needs backup," Master Shifu said.

Po's eyes widened. "Ooh! Dragon Warrior stealth mode!"

He hurried after Mantis, hiding behind trees so that the tiny warrior wouldn't spot him. But Po's stealth mode wasn't exactly quiet. Every time he jumped from tree to tree, he made grunting noises. It wasn't long before Mantis figured out he was being followed.

The little insect grabbed Po's left foot and flipped him onto his belly.

"Talk!" Mantis commanded.

"Shifu wanted me to follow you," Po said. "Guess he thought something was up."

Mantis sighed. "There's something I need to tell you," he said. "A few years ago, Hao Ming left me at the altar."

"Did she forget something?" Po asked.

Mantis's eyes welled with tears. "My heart."

"Your teeny-tiny little heart?" Po asked.

Mantis nodded. "I was out of my mind."

"Your teeny-tiny little mind?" Po asked.

"I wanted her to regret it, so I told a lie," Mantis admitted.

"A teeny-tiny little—" Po started to say.

"I get it! I'm small!" Mantis yelled.

Suddenly a group of excited villagers came running down the path.

"It's the Dragon Warrior!" one of them yelled.

Po opened his paws, waiting to greet them. But they ran right past them. They picked up Mantis, placed him on a tiny chair, and carried him into the village.

"Long live the Dragon Warrior!" they cheered.

CHAPTER **TWO**

The villagers danced a happy jig in the square to welcome the Dragon Warrior. Po walked up to Mantis.

"So, buddy, anything you wanted to tell me?" Po asked.

Mantis sighed. "I wanted to seem like a big shot so I could burn my ex-fiancée for dumping me. So I told everyone I was the Dragon Warrior."

He pointed to a mantis in the crowd of

dancers. Long eyelashes fluttered on her eye-lids. Her back was painted with pretty flowers.

"There she is!" he said. "I'll tell everyone the truth as soon as they're done, even if she does see that I'm a total loser."

Po felt bad for his friend. "Or, you could just keep on being the Dragon Warrior. I give you per-mission to be me. And to rub her tiny little nose in it."

Mantis hopped into Po's paw. "That would be really great! But if I'm the Dragon Warrior, who are you?"

"Your sidekick!" Po suggested. "There's just one problem. I have to find a way to hide my natural bodacity. I need a costume."

Po went off in search of something to wear and returned just in time for the feast in the Dragon Warrior's honor.

"Please welcome the Dragon Warrior!" Mayor Pig announced to the villagers gathered in the banquet hall.

They cheered as two geese carried in Mantis on his chair.

"And his . . . sidekick," Mayor Pig said.

Po walked in, limping, with a crutch in one paw and an eye patch on his eye. He banged into the doorway.

"Greetings all. *Flaaarp!*" he cried, waving to the villagers with his crutch.

He sat down next to Mantis, who gave him a curious look.

"Thought I'd add some weird noises to the sidekick thing," Po whispered.

Hao Ming hopped over to Mantis's chair and bowed.

"So nice to see you again, Dragon Warrior," she said.

Mantis pretended not to remember her. "Oh, hello, Miss . . . ?"

"Hao," she said.

"Ah, yes, Hao. I think I got one of your urgent messages," Mantis said. "It was in a pile of urgent messages."

"It was an urgent message. It was more about me urgently missing you," she said. "There's an

empty seat next to mine, Dragon Warrior."

Mantis hopped off his chair and went to sit next to her, winking at Po. Hao Ming thought he was awesome! Their plan was working.

"I have always regretted leaving you," Hao told Mantis. "You were the most—"

"I love you too!" Mantis blurted out.

"Take that!" Po cried. "Wait, what?" Mantis was supposed to be making Hao feel bad—not taking her back.

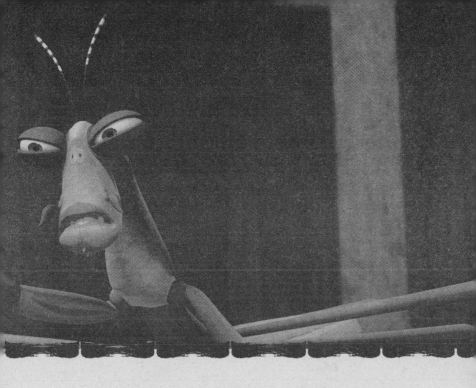

"Will you have this humble hero as your boy-friend?" Mantis continued.

"Yes!" Hao cried.

Suddenly an angry red mantis leaped onto the table.

"Liar!" he yelled, pointing at Mantis. "Fraud! You're no hero!"

CHAPTER **THREE**

Mantis gasped. His secret was out!

"I can explain . . . ," he began, but the red mantis wouldn't let him.

"You say you're the Dragon Warrior, but you're really . . . a girlfriend thief!" the red mantis accused.

Mantis turned to his girlfriend. "Who is this old guy?"

"Uh, that's Dosu, my ex-fiancé," she explained with a shrug.

"When did you break up?" Mantis asked.

"Two hours and seventeen minutes ago," Dosu said sadly. "Because of *you*, Dragon Warrior!"

"Because I realized the truth of me loving you," Hao explained.

"Because you're the Dragon Warrior!" Dosu yelled, pointing at Mantis.

"Not true," Hao protested. "I love Mantis for who he is."

Then a goat with a gray beard stomped up to Po.

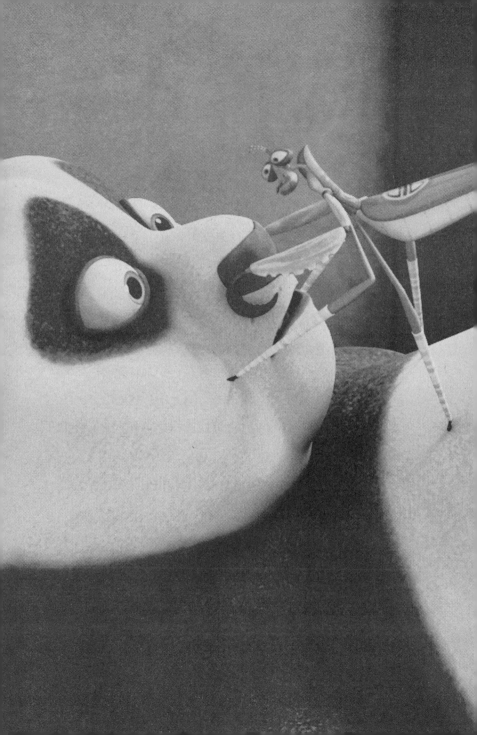

"You're gonna be sorry," he said, glaring up at him.

"Who are you?" Po asked.

"I'm Sai So, Dosu's sidekick," the goat answered.

"We challenge you and your sidekick to a fight so we know who the *real* hero is," Dosu said, pointing at Mantis. "Tomorrow. Noon. The town square. Don't be late."

That night, Mantis climbed onto Po's belly as Po snuggled into his cot.

"Hao likes me, Po!" Mantis said. "She's crazy about me. I'm in love!"

Po was worried about the fight tomorrow. "I can't fight those guys. If I start fighting them, they'll figure out that *I'm* the Dragon Warrior, and *you're* not."

"That can't happen!" Mantis wailed. "Po, I'll be there."

But the next day at noon, there was no sign of Mantis.

"I'm sure he'll be here," Po said nervously. "Probably caught up doing something awesome. *Glooorp!*"

Then the clocked chimed twelve.

Pow! Sai So hurled himself at Po and started pummeling his face.

Bam! Dosu flipped Po back and forth like a rag doll.

Po didn't fight back.

Dosu finally hopped off Po. "Tell the Dragon Warrior we'll be back here at two. He better show up . . . if he knows what's good for him."

Po went back to the hut. Mantis bounded in, humming a happy tune. He stopped when he saw Po, who looked a little rough after the fight.

"What happened?" Mantis asked.

"There was a fight? At noon?" Po reminded him.

"I'm sorry, Po! I'm a little goofy on love," Mantis explained. "Are you okay?"

"Nothing hurt but my pride . . . and a couple of ribs," Po said. "But you can do me a solid by kicking those guys' butts at two o'clock."

"You can count on me, pal!" Mantis said.

But two o'clock came . . . and Mantis didn't show . . . again.

Pow! Bam! Crunch! Dosu and Sai So wiped the square with Po . . . again.

Back at the hut, Mantis saw an upset and beat-up Po. He had been out with Hao again.

"I can do six!" Mantis declared.

But six o'clock came . . . and for the third time, Mantis didn't show.

Pow! Bam! Crunch! Dosu and Sai So kept pounding Po, and Po kept acting like he couldn't fight.

Hours later, Po limped through the door of the

hut. Mantis bounded past him, humming another happy tune.

"Po, is it six o'clock already?" Mantis asked.

"It's nine," Po said with a groan.

"Hey, you actually look like you need that crutch now," Mantis remarked.

"I do," Po said.

"Aw, I'm sorry," Mantis said. "Look, next time . . ."

"There's not gonna be a next time!" Po yelled. "You're a disgrace to the Dragon Warrior name! The Dragon Warrior is supposed to be there for those who need him. Not just think about himself."

"Po!" Mantis cried.

"Don't 'Po' me, Mantis," Po said, pointing at Mantis. The crutch slipped out from under Po's arm, and he fell flat on his face. He groaned. "As soon as I get my sight back, I'm leaving!"

CHAPTER **FOUR**

"What? No! Please! Not now!" Mantis begged.

"Because?" Po asked.

"Because Hao and I are getting married!" Mantis cried.

"Are you out of your mind?" Po asked. "You were just going to make her a little jealous and then skedaddle. This is all a lie!"

"I'll tell her the truth eventually," Mantis promised. "Shouldn't be more than a few years."

Po sighed. "No more, Mantis. I'm going

home." He limped out of the hut, muttering to himself. "Try to help a guy out. What does it get ya? Butt-kickings and a big mouthful of disappointment . . . but with less teeth."

He made his way into the bamboo forest. "Let's see that red mantis dude and his sidekick take me on when I'm really trying. *Aiiyahh*!"

He threw away the crutch, slicing off the tops of some bamboo stalks. Then he launched into the air, kicking every stalk in the clearing with his powerful feet. When he settled back down, every stalk toppled around him, kicking up dust from the sandy ground.

"Say hello to the Dragon Warrior!" he cried. It

felt good to be acting awesome again.

Then he looked down—and saw Dosu and Sai So staring up at him.

"Wait, *you're* the Dragon Warrior?" Dosu asked.

"We have to tell Hao she's marrying a fraud!" Sai So yelled.

Dosu and Sai So started hurrying back to the village.

Po ran after them. Even though Mantis had let him down, he didn't want to see his friend get hurt.

Back in the village square, the wedding had already started. Mantis and Hao stood in front of Mayor Pig.

Dosu hopped into the square. "Hao Ming! I have some interesting news for you about your Dragon—"

Whomp! Po pretended to accidentally step on Dosu. Then he waved to the mayor. "Keep going!"

"This guy is not the Dragon—" Sai So began, but Po quickly rolled over on him before he could finish.

"Dragon Warrior, you may now say your vows," Mayor Pig said.

Mantis unrolled a long scroll. He looked into

Hao's eyes. "Remember when I was four and you were three?"

With a mighty grunt, Dosu pushed Po off and jumped free. "Fraud!" he said as Po picked him up and squeezed him inside his paw.

"Weddings always make me cry," Po said. "Let's just hold each other for a minute."

Then Hao began her vows. "My dearest Dragon Warrior," she said. In the background, Mantis could

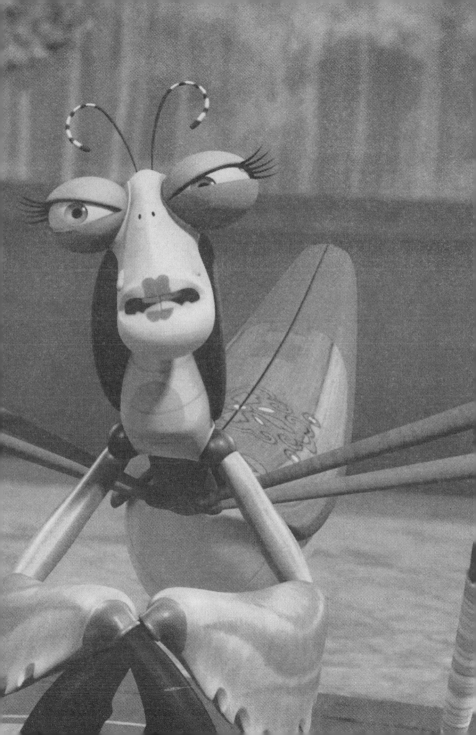

hear Po fighting Dosu and Sai So. "Since the day I first heard there was a Dragon Warrior, I knew I wanted to be Mrs. Dragon Warrior."

Dragon Warrior . . . Dragon Warrior . . . something clicked inside Mantis's head. Hao didn't love

him for who he was. She just wanted to be with the Dragon Warrior. And that was Po. And Po needed him right now.

The foggy cloud of love lifted.

"No!" Mantis shouted.

CHAPTER **FIVE**

M antis launched himself into the air.
Bam! He hit Sai So with a powerful kick.
The goat went flying.

Then Mantis hopped over to Po. Dosu had slammed Po into the ground and stood on Po's back.

"Get off my friend," Mantis growled.

Dosu let out a battle cry and jumped off Po.

Clash! Slash! Mantis and Dosu traded kung-fu blows.

Mantis jumped back. He leaped toward Dosu, kicking him with his two back legs. Then he grabbed Dosu by the head and spun him around and around.

"Whoa!" Dosu flew across the square and landed right in front of Hao.

"Mantis is not the Dragon Warrior," he said, as he panted for air.

"Then who is?" Hao asked.

Dosu pointed to Po. "That guy!" he cried, and the villagers gasped.

"What? Me?" Po said. "I can't even walk. *Blaargh!*"

"Stop!" Mantis cried. "I can't watch you do this,

86

Po. Everyone, I am *not* the Dragon Warrior!"

"The wedding is off," Hao said, but Mantis didn't care.

"Not only am I not the Dragon Warrior, I am not *worthy* to be him," Mantis told the crowd. He pointed to Po. "*That* guy is worthy. He's my best friend. He took several beatings and humiliated himself, even more than usual, just so I could marry a woman who doesn't even deserve me."

"I don't deserve *you*? You don't deserve *me*!" Hao said, and hopped off in a huff. Dosu ran after her and gave her a big hug. Now that Hao Ming was single, maybe they could be together again!

Po and Mantis said good-bye to the villagers and headed home. Poor Po was having a tough time. He grunted with each step.

"Po, get on my shoulders," Mantis said.

Mantis scuttled underneath Po.

Squash! Po sat right on top of Mantis. But the strong little warrior pushed up with all his might. He held Po by Po's legs and carried him down the path.

The two friends headed back into the bamboo forest, back to the Jade Palace . . . and their next adventure.